The Dog Hole

Ricky Ke

Published and distributed by Gatehouse Books Ltd
Hulme Adult Education Centre, Stretford Road,
Manchester M15 5FQ
ISBN 1 84231 006 2
British Library cataloguing in publication data:
A catalogue record for this book is available from the
British Library

Editor, Patricia Duffin
Writers in Residence at HMYOI Swinfen Hall, Maria Whatton, Jan Watts
Resource Centre Manager at HMYOI Swinfen Hall, Rachael Cranley
Illustrations and cover design, Ivor Arbuckle
Printed by RAP Ltd, Oldham

This book is a further title in The CoolBooks series. The CoolBooks Project
was a partnership between Gatehouse Publishing Charity Ltd and the Writers
in Prison Network, telephone 01938 811355.

The CoolBooks Project is grateful for the support of Governors and staff at
HMP/YOI Foston Hall, HMYOI Glen Parva, HMP/YOI Styal and HMYOI
Swinfen Hall and for their opinions and comments to the prisoners and staff
who made up the Reading Circles, who recommended this book for publication.

Gatehouse acknowledges grant aid towards the production of this book from
The Ernest Cook Trust.

Gatehouse provides an opportunity for writers to express their thoughts and
feelings on aspects of their lives. The views expressed are not necessarily
those of Gatehouse.

Gatehouse Books

Books by and for adult learners

The **CoolBooks** pilot project is a partnership between The Gatehouse Publishing Charity and The Writers in Prisons *Network*. Writing workshops aimed at prisoners with basic skills needs were set up and co-run by Writers in residence and Gatehouse staff using a range of methods to stimulate and develop writing. The writing was then passed to *reading circles* which again comprised prisoners with basic skills needs. The groups met over several sessions to choose the texts which would go forward for piloting as a book.

Who are Gatehouse?

Gatehouse is a unique Manchester based community publisher. · We have been publishing books for adults with reading and writing difficulties for the past 25 years. Uniquely in publishing, Gatehouse authors are themselves adult learners who are developing their reading and writing skills. At Gatehouse we believe that the best people to write for adult learners are those who have been through the same experience themselves. So Gatehouse books speak of an experience that readers can understand and share. If you enjoyed this book then we are sure you will enjoy many of the Gatehouse titles.

The best day was Friday, wages day.
All the bin men were there
waiting for their wages, and larking about.
One Friday, three of us went in the yard
and saw two legs
sticking out of one of the wagons.
Have you ever seen artificial legs?
They look so real.
And these had trousers on, and shoes!

20

extract from 'The Bin Men'

Booklist Available

Gatehouse Books
Hulme Adult Education Centre
Stretford Road
Manchester M15 5FQ
Tel: 0161 226 7152
E-mail: office@gatehousebooks.org.uk
www.gatehousebooks.org.uk

3

Introduction

This book is dedicated to Gemma and Dylan.

My life is about to change.
It's a new start.
I am looking to see what happens
when I get out there.
Back outside. Back in Birmingham.
I didn't plan the book
it just happened.
All the computers in the library were full
and Maria asked me about a story
when I was younger
and this is it.
Everybody has stories to tell.
You could tell yours too.

Ricky Kennedy

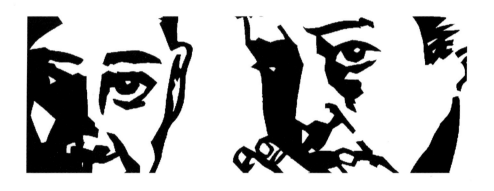

I went to school with Morgan.

He was in my class.

One day he said,

"Do you wanna come back to mine?

I've asked my mum.

She said she'll do some tea."

Now, I thought his mum
would do the same as mine,
things like waffles, chips or beans,
but I was to find out different.

We went back

in his mum's car,

which sounded like a tank.

When we got there, his mum said,

"You can go and play when we get in."

From the outside,

it was a normal terraced house

on a council estate,

but then she opened the front door.

There was a hallway with stairs.

I had never seen anything like it before.

I had never been in a house

so written-off as this.

There was a coat rack on the wall,
but all the coats were on the floor
with bags on them.
There were shoes and trainers
scattered along the corridor.

It was like an obstacle course
and we had to hop over everything
to get to the living room.

As soon as we walked in there
I didn't know where to sit.
There was a quilt on the settee
and a pile of washing on a chair
that looked like they had got it
off the line and flung it.

It looked like a dog basket
with a tramp sleeping inside.
If someone had come in
to burgle it
they would have gone out
thinking it had already been done over!

It smelt like they had a damp dog.

It smelt mouldy.

The funny thing was

they didn't have a dog.

I could smell sweaty socks.

I felt really funny.

If my room had been like that,

my mum would have given me

a boot up the arse.

We did go and play

on his computer for a while

when his mum was cooking the tea.

I could smell it,

and I made a couple of excuses.

It was winter time,
so I said,"It's getting dark,
I have got to go."

I walked home.

When I got in

I compared Morgan's house with mine.

Mine was a palace in comparison.

I was really glad I had my mum

instead of his.

Cool*Books*

new fiction for adult learners in prison written *by* and *for* offenders

Other books in the Cool*Books* series include:-

'The Cool*Books* File' - to enable those working in prisons to create further prison specific resources.